The Jenny Summer

by Carol Greene

illustrated by Ellen Eagle

Harper & Row, Publishers

For Nat and Julie

Library of Congress Cataloging-in-Publication Data
Greene, Carol.
    The Jenny summer.

    Summary: When a new family with a girl her age moves
in next door, Robin discovers the pleasure of having a
best friend and the pain of losing her.
    [1. Friendship—Fiction]   I. Eagle, Ellen, ill.
II. Title.
PZ7.G82845Je 1988   [Fic]   87-45283
    ISBN 0-06-022208-5
    ISBN 0-06-022209-3 (lib. bdg.)

CONTENTS

O N E

Buried Treasure

"I'm bored," said Robin Hill.

"You can't be," said her mother. She was reading the newspaper at the kitchen table. "School has been out only a week."

"I know," said Robin. "But I'm bored anyway. Can't we do something exciting—like go to the zoo?"

"Sorry." Her mother turned a page. "I don't have the car today. And you know what happens to Danny on the bus."

"Yeah." Robin sighed. Danny was her little brother. Sometimes he threw up on busses. "Well, can we make our own zoo

1

in the living room? You know, turn the furniture over and—"

"We *can*," said her mother. "But we aren't going to. I just cleaned in there."

"Oh." Robin thought for a minute. "Would you like to play bears with me under the kitchen table?"

"I'd *like* to read this paper, Robin. Why don't you play with your kitten?"

Robin frowned. "Pottsy is taking her one millionth nap of the day."

"Then why don't you clean out your closet?" said her mother. "You haven't touched it for months. Maybe you'll find buried treasure. *That* would be exciting."

"Oh, *Mom!*" said Robin. But she went to her room and opened the closet door. Then she dragged over a chair to stand on.

I really haven't looked on the top shelf for a long time, she thought.

She found last summer's sneakers, an

old Easter hat, and a pink purse with a duck on it.

The Goodwill would like this stuff, she decided. She dropped it in a pile on the floor.

Next she found an empty goldfish bowl. Poor Bubbles, she thought. The landlady, Mrs. Potts, had accidentally killed him. That was why she had given Pottsy to Robin. But it still made Robin sad to see Bubbles' bowl. She tried to push it farther back on the shelf.

It wouldn't go. Something was in the way. Robin reached around to see what it was. She pulled out a white box.

That's strange, she thought. I don't remember this box.

She got down and opened it. Inside was a red book. It had a funny little flap with a lock. Across the front was the word "Diary."

Now I remember! Robin thought.

Grandma Bennett gave me this a long time ago. I couldn't write very well then. So Mom put it away until I was older. This really *is* like finding buried treasure!

She pushed the chair back to her desk and sat down. On the first page of the diary she printed the date. Then she wrote:

Dear Diary,

This morning I got up. I ate breakfast. I played jacks outside. I played with Danny inside. I ate lunch. Then I cleaned out my closet. That is when I found you. Now I will write in you every day.

But what will I say? she wondered. All I do is the same old things. Even a diary will get bored with them. I wonder what interesting people write in their diaries. People like princesses—

She stared at the wall for a minute.

Then she turned to the next page and wrote:

Dearest Diary,
    Today I rose from my silk couch. I ate raspberries and cream. Then I rode my milk-white stallion. Forty of my friends came to lunch. We ate lobsters. Then we danced in the ballroom. We swam in my pearl-lined pool. We—

Robin stopped. Boy, I wish I had forty friends, she thought. I wish I had *one* friend. Maybe then I wouldn't be so bored.
    Just then the phone rang.

T W O

An Invitation

Good, thought Robin when she heard the phone. Maybe that's Daddy. Maybe he's coming home early, and we can go to the zoo.

"Robin!" called her mother. "It's for you."

"Me?" said Robin. She hurried to the kitchen and picked up the receiver. "Hello?"

"Hi, Robin," said a voice. "This is Melissa Berger. You know, from school? Uh—I wondered if you could come over tomorrow for lunch. Then we could play in the afternoon."

"Oh," said Robin. "Just a minute. I'll ask my mom."

"Of course you may go," said Mrs. Hill. "Tell Melissa that I'll walk you over about noon."

"Wow!" said Robin when she'd hung up. "I was just wishing I had a friend. Now maybe I've got one."

Her mother smiled. "Maybe you do."

That night Robin wrote in her diary again:

Today turned out okay.
I *may* have a friend.

The next day she and her mother walked to Melissa's house. It was only two blocks away. Mrs. Hill pushed Danny in his stroller.

"You know, Mom, I'm kind of nervous," said Robin. "I sure hope Melissa likes me."

"She does like you, honey," said her

mother. "That's why she called you. Just be sure and remember your manners."

"I will," promised Robin. She'd looked through her manners book right after breakfast. If she was *extra* polite, maybe Melissa would want to be her friend for good.

Melissa was waiting at the front door. She lived in an upstairs flat too.

"Hi, Robin!" she said. "Come on up. Lunch is ready. We're having peanut-butter sandwiches and carrot sticks."

"How delicious," said Robin politely. " 'Bye, Mom. See you at four."

It wasn't hard to use her best manners at lunch. There weren't even any forks to worry about. She remembered to wipe her mouth with her napkin too.

"Thank you for a lovely meal, Mrs. Berger," she said.

"Would you like to play jacks now, Robin?" asked Melissa.

"That would be nice," said Robin. "But I didn't bring mine."

"Oh, that's okay," said Melissa. "We can share mine."

They took the jacks down to the backyard. Melissa was very good at pigs-in-a-pen. But Robin was better at eggs-in-a-basket. They each won two games. Then they played hopscotch.

"This is fun," said Melissa. "I was getting bored with summer vacation. My mom said I was driving her crazy."

"Yeah." Robin moved her rock to the third space. "I think my mom felt that way too."

At four o'clock, Mrs. Hill rang the doorbell.

"Thank you for having me, Mrs. Berger," said Robin. "And thank you, Melissa."

"You're welcome," said Melissa. "I'm glad you could come."

That night Robin wrote in her diary:

Dear Diary,

Today I went to Melissa Berger's. We ate and played games. I remembered my manners. I think Melissa will be my friend.

She started to close the diary. Then she saw a little envelope stuck inside the back cover. In it was a small gold key.

I wonder if I should lock my diary, she thought. But who would read it? Mom and Daddy are honest. They know diaries are private. And Danny can't read at all.

So she put the key back inside the envelope and closed the diary.

THREE

Melissa Sleeps Over

The next day Robin decided to invite Melissa to visit her.

"See if she can come to dinner tomorrow evening," said Mrs. Hill. "Then we'll all go to a movie. If you like, you may ask her to spend the night too."

"Wow!" said Robin. She dialed Melissa's number.

"I'd love to come," said Melissa. *"Achoo!"*

"You aren't getting sick, are you?" asked Robin. It would be awful if Melissa got sick and couldn't come after all.

"No." Melissa sniffled. "It's just my allergy. I forgot to take a pill today."

13

"Oh," said Robin. "Well, don't forget to take one tomorrow. And don't forget your sleeping bag."

"I won't," said Melissa. " 'Bye, Robin."

It seemed like forever until tomorrow. Robin cleaned her room. She played in the backyard six times. She got out the clothes she wanted to wear the next day. Then she put them back and got out different ones.

"Tomorrow is never going to come," she wrote in her diary.

But it did. At five-thirty the next day, Mr. Berger brought Melissa, her backpack, and her sleeping bag.

"Hi," said Robin. "Let me carry something. We're having *pizza* for dinner."

"Great!" said Melissa.

It turned out that she liked the same kind of pizza as Robin—with hamburger and lots of cheese.

"My dad likes anchovies and olives," she said. "Isn't that *sickening*?"

"Ugh!" said Robin.

They both liked the movie too.

"Dog movies are the best kind in the world," said Robin.

"Yep," said Melissa. "And people who are mean to dogs should be sent to desert islands."

"Forever," said Robin.

While Melissa brushed her teeth, Robin wrote in her diary:

> Everything is great. Melissa and I like the same things. More later.

I wonder if we'll giggle all night, she thought. That's what you're supposed to do when a friend sleeps over.

"Sweet dreams, girls," said Mrs. Hill. She turned out the light and closed the door.

"Melissa?" whispered Robin. "Do you know any good jokes?"

"Let me think," whispered Melissa.

Robin waited a long time. Then she heard a funny noise. It was Melissa. She was snoring.

The next morning Robin stirred the orange juice while Melissa rolled up her sleeping bag. When all the orange lumps were gone, Robin went back to the bedroom.

"Here I am," she said. "I— What are you *doing*?"

There sat Melissa in the middle of the floor. She was reading Robin's diary.

"Nothing!" Melissa slammed shut the diary and jumped up. "I—uh—just found this book. I thought I'd see what it was."

"You *know* what it is!" Robin was so angry that her voice squeaked. "It says 'Diary' right on the front. You were reading my diary! That's the worst thing anyone can do!"

"Aw, come on, Robin." Melissa looked scared now. "I only saw one little bit.

Something about a princess—"

"Oooo!" Robin wanted to say, "I hate you. Get out of my house." But she knew she mustn't. Melissa was still her guest. So she grabbed the diary and stuck it under her pillow.

"Breakfast is ready," she said. "You go first." Then she closed her bedroom door behind them.

All through breakfast Robin remembered her manners. She talked about the weather. She told her mother the scrambled eggs were delicious. At last Mr. Berger came for Melissa. Robin carried her sleeping bag to the car.

"Thank you for inviting me, Robin," said Melissa. "I—"

"You're welcome," said Robin. She went back inside and up the stairs.

"Well," said her father. "Does my Mousie have a best friend now?"

"No!" said Robin. "I never want to see Melissa Berger again as long as I live!"

FOUR

A Visit and Two Surprises

It took Robin a long time to tell her parents what Melissa had done. She was so angry that she kept crying. But at last she got the whole story out.

"I thought Melissa was my *friend*," she sniffed. "But friends don't do sneaky things like that."

"Oh, Robin." Her mother hugged her. "Sometimes friends make mistakes."

"But this wasn't a mistake," said Robin. "Melissa read my diary on *purpose*."

"I suppose she did." Mrs. Hill sighed. "But—oh, never mind." She turned to

19

Robin's father. "I think it's time for what we talked about last week."

Mr. Hill nodded. "I'll go call."

"Call? Call who? Time for what?" Robin scrubbed the last tears off her face with her hands.

"Daddy and I thought you might like to spend a few days with Grandma Bennett," said her mother. "What do you think?"

"I think I'd *love* it!" All at once Robin felt much better. Grandma Bennett lived in a big old house in the suburbs. She and Robin always had a great time together.

"All set," said Mr. Hill a few minutes later. "Grandma said to bring you out this very afternoon."

"Super!" said Robin. "I'll go pack."

That night Robin lay in Grandma Bennett's pink guest room. Grandma sat on the edge of the bed. She had a book in her lap.

"You don't have to read to me, Grandma," said Robin. "I can read very well by myself. Honest!"

"Hush," said Grandma. "It is my *right* as a grandmother to read to you. So be quiet and listen."

Robin grinned and snuggled down. Phooey on Melissa Berger! she thought. Who needs her?

The next morning Grandma took her to the Episcopal church.

"We don't kneel at our church," whispered Robin during the prayers. "I like it. It makes me feel holy."

"It makes me feel stiff," Grandma whispered back. "But holy too."

After church they went to a restaurant in a supermarket for brunch.

"Grandma?" said Robin. "Do you think God wants me to forgive Melissa Berger?"

"Well—" Grandma took a sip of coffee. "I imagine He'd like it. Why? Are you having trouble?"

"I sure am." Robin sighed. "How much time do you think He'll give me?"

"As much as you need," said Grandma. "He's very patient."

In the afternoon they worked in the

garden. Robin pulled up all the pesky little weeds. Grandma said that was as good as a vacation for her knees.

"I was just about ready to send them to Arizona," she said.

Robin giggled.

The next day they went to the zoo. The day after that they visited the planetarium. Then Grandma took Robin shopping. She bought her two shorts sets and a little china cat. Robin bought Grandma a pink plastic rose. It didn't cost much. But it was beautiful.

Much too soon the time came for Robin to go home.

"I wish we lived next door to Grandma," she said in the car. "Then we could do lots more things together. And I could help her."

"Grandma said you were a big help, Goosefeather," said her father. "I'm proud of you. Maybe you can visit again later this summer."

"But right now," said her mother, "there are two surprises for you at home."

"Two?" Robin sat up straight. "What are they?"

"Wait and see," said her mother.

Robin found the first surprise right away. It was an envelope on her desk. Inside was a card with real pressed flowers on it. On the back someone had written, "From your Secret Pal."

"Who is it?" asked Robin. "Do you know, Mom? Daddy?"

"I haven't the foggiest," said her father.

"You aren't supposed to know who your secret pal is," said her mother. "That's the whole point. I had one for a whole year when I was a little girl. It turned out to be an old lady at my church."

"Wow!" said Robin. "I'm going to put this on my bulletin board."

"Don't you want to know about the other surprise?" asked her father.

"Sure!" said Robin. "What is it?"

"Well, a new family has moved into that empty flat in the next building. And—" Her father waited until Robin thought she'd burst. "And they have a girl just your age."

F I V E

Jenny

"What's her name? What's she like? Are there any other kids?" Questions bubbled up in Robin.

"Help!" said her father. "I don't know. I just met her father taking out the trash. Their last name is O'Rourke. You'll have to wait till tomorrow for the rest, Froggie."

Robin thought she'd never get to sleep that night. Then she overslept the next morning. It was after ten when she hurried into the kitchen.

"I think I'll go hang around in the backyard, Mom," she said.

"Not without your cereal," said her mother.

So Robin gulped down a bowl of cornflakes and some orange juice. Then she picked up Pottsy and headed for the door.

"Be careful with her," said Mrs. Hill. "Remember, she's not an outdoors cat."

"I know," said Robin. "I just want her along in case the new girl and I don't know what to talk about."

"Good idea," said her mother.

Robin saw the girl right away. She was sitting on the step outside her door. Her red hair hid her face. But Robin could see that she was holding something in her lap.

Robin took a deep breath. Then she walked over and leaned against the fence.

"Hi," she said.

The girl didn't move.

Rats! thought Robin. She took another deep breath. "I said 'hi'!" she yelled.

"Oh!" The girl jumped up. Three teddy

bears fell off her lap. She bent over and picked them up. "Hi. I didn't hear you the first time."

Robin nodded. "I thought you didn't. My name is Robin Hill. This is my kitten, Pottsy. I like your bears."

"I'm Jenny O'Rourke," said the girl. "And these are the Gumbo bears. They're my best friends."

"What's a Gumbo bear?" asked Robin.

"Oh, a bear that's soft and squishy and—I don't know. I just call them that." Jenny held up the bears one at a time. "This is Big Gumbo. This is Middle Gumbo. And this is Little Gumbo."

"They're *adorable*," said Robin. "I used to have a bear when I was little. But Mom tried to wash it. It wasn't a washing kind of bear. We had to get a man to fix the machine and everything."

"Wow!" said Jenny. "Hey, Robin, I'll let you hold the Gumbos if you'll let me hold your kitten."

"Okay," said Robin. "Only don't let her get away."

It was not easy to get three bears across the fence one way and one kitten the other. Somehow, Middle Gumbo ended up in a rosebush. And Pottsy ended up loose.

"Oh, no!" yelled Robin.

"Don't worry!" yelled Jenny. "I'll catch her."

But Pottsy had other ideas. Back and forth along the fence she darted. Sometimes she was on Jenny's side. Sometimes she scooted under to Robin's. Soon both girls were panting and giggling so hard they couldn't talk.

At last Pottsy sat down to wash her face.

"Gotcha!" yelled Jenny. "Look, now she's washing *my* face. What a crazy cat!"

"Yeah." Robin reached over and scratched Pottsy's ears. "Where did you live before?"

"In Chicago." All at once Jenny looked

sad. "I didn't want to move. Everything is in Chicago. My school, my friends, my grandparents—everything. But my dad got a new job."

"Wow!" said Robin softly. She thought about how much *she'd* hate to move. "That's really tough. But your parents are here."

"Yeah." Jenny frowned. Then she smiled. "And so are you. I never lived next door to a kid my own age before."

"Me either." Robin smiled too. "I'll bet there are a million things we can do together."

"*Two* million," said Jenny. "Do you like to—"

"Jenny!" called a woman's voice. "Lunch is ready."

"Gotta go." Carefully Jenny handed Pottsy back over the fence. Robin tucked the kitten under one arm. Then she handed back the Gumbo bears.

Jenny ran to the back door. Her hair

streamed out behind her. Then she stopped and turned.

"See you this afternoon, Robin?" she asked.

"See you this afternoon," said Robin. She hurried upstairs too.

"Mom! *Mom!*" she shouted. "I've got a super new friend!"

S I X

Special Magic

Robin gobbled down her own lunch. Jenny's probably done already, she kept thinking. She's probably waiting for me.

But when she got downstairs, Jenny wasn't there. So Robin began to throw an old tennis ball against the garage.

When I catch it ten times in a row, Jenny will come, she decided.

She was up to eight when the ball hit a crack. Under the Pottses' back porch it flew.

Rats! thought Robin. She crawled after it. When she came back out, Jenny stood at the fence. She was laughing.

"Is that where you live?" she asked.

"Yep." Robin giggled. "We've got a ballroom and a swimming pool and everything under there."

"Hey, look." Jenny reached across the fence and picked something out of Robin's hair. "It's a spider."

"Yuck!" Robin shook her head as hard as she could. "Squash it!"

"Why?" Jenny put the spider on the sidewalk. "It's a perfectly nice spider."

"Boy, you're brave," said Robin.

"Nope," said Jenny. "I just like things to be alive." They watched the spider scurry away.

"I'll bet it's going home to tell its children about its adventure," said Robin. "Want to come upstairs and meet my mother?"

"Sure."

Jenny said a polite hello to Mrs. Hill. Then she saw Danny. He was sitting on the kitchen floor chewing his blanket.

Jenny squatted down right beside him.

"Hi, you," she said. "What a bunch of curls!" She patted Danny's yellow head. "You feel almost as good as a Gumbo bear."

Danny stared at her. Then he held out his blanket.

"Boop," he said.

"That's his blanket's name," explained Robin. "He won't let most people *touch* it. He must really like you."

"Do you have any brothers or sisters, Jenny?" asked Mrs. Hill.

"No, ma'am," said Jenny. "Just me."

"Want to see my room?" asked Robin.

She showed Jenny her diary, too. Then she told her what Melissa had done.

"I guess that's sort of a secret," she said. "If you ever meet Melissa, don't tell her I told you."

"I won't," promised Jenny. "I'll tell you a secret too. Sometimes at night my folks have fights and I can't sleep. So I say 'George Washington, George Washington' over and over again. You know, inside my head. It's got a good rhythm. I almost always fall asleep. Do you think that's dumb?"

"No," said Robin. "I think it's very smart. I'll try it the next time I can't sleep."

It must be awful to hear your parents fighting at night, she thought. But she didn't say anything about that.

From then on, Robin and Jenny spent every minute they could together. Robin's father even helped them loop a long piece of clothesline between their back porches. He attached a basket to the line with a big clip.

"Now you can send messages back and forth, Goosefeather," he said.

"And other stuff too," added Robin. She ran inside and came back with a banana to send Jenny.

"Hey, thanks!" said Jenny with her mouth full. Then she sent a book across to Robin.

"It's *Bambi*," she said. "The real one, not the cartoon. You can borrow it."

"Okay," said Robin. "I'll lend you *Sarah, Plain and Tall*. It's terrific."

"I wonder if the Post Office will sue me," said Mr. Hill.

One day Melissa called. She wanted Robin to spend the night with her.

"I'm sorry, Melissa," said Robin. "I'm really busy this summer. Thanks for asking me, though."

She didn't exactly hate Melissa anymore. But she'd rather be with Jenny.

That night Robin lay in bed reading *Bambi*. After a while her mother came in to say good night.

"I wish I were a deer," sighed Robin. "Deer are so beautiful."

Her mother smiled. "I'd rather be a dear mama than a mama deer," she said.

Robin sat up. "Wow, Mom! That was a clever thing to say."

"Thank you. Are you ready to go to sleep now?"

"I guess so." Robin lay down again. "Mom, do you think that sometimes magic happens between people? Special magic that makes them instant friends?"

Her mother thought for a moment. "I don't know if it's magic, Robin. But I know what you mean. The same thing happened with me and my friend Gwen when we were your age."

"And you're still friends now," said Robin. "Even if Gwen does live in Philadelphia."

That made her feel good. Maybe she and Jenny would be friends forever too.

SEVEN

Hats

Robin and Jenny decided to call their clothesline the Basket Express. Each girl checked it several times a day. If the basket was on her side, almost anything could be in it.

Once Jenny sent Robin a plastic spider. With it was a tag. It said: "Folks with eight legs need love too."

Robin knew just what to send back. She spent all afternoon trying to make a web out of yarn. At last she wrote in her diary:

I give up. When it comes to webs,
spiders are smarter than I am.

One rainy morning she sent Jenny a
note in a plastic bag.

*Please come over and play. My
mom will feed you lunch.*

Ten minutes later, Jenny knocked at
the back door. She wore an old rain hat.
But the rest of her was dripping wet.

"Don't you have an umbrella?" asked
Robin.

"Oh, it got lost when we moved." Jenny
didn't sound worried.

"Well, put on some of Robin's things
while I dry yours," said Mrs. Hill. "There's
nothing worse than a summer cold."

"I thought we could make pretty-
pretties today," said Robin. Jenny was
putting on her old yellow T-shirt.

"Pretty-pretties?" Jenny asked. "What's a pretty-pretty?"

Robin felt her face get warm. "They're like designs. You take a black crayon and scribble on a piece of paper. Then you make the scribble shapes bright colors and the border black. I made up the name when I was a little kid. Dumb, huh?"

"I think it sounds like fun," said Jenny.

Robin smiled. She never thinks I'm dumb, she thought. And I never think she is.

They made several pretty-pretties and stuck them on the refrigerator. Then Robin's mother asked her to go downstairs for the mail.

"Look!" Robin galloped back up the steps. "A package for me. I'll bet it's from my secret pal."

She tore open the small brown mailer. Inside, wrapped in tissue paper, was a little tin donkey. It wore a huge sombrero.

"It's a pin, Robin," said Jenny. "From
Mexico, I'll bet. Isn't it precious? Here,
let me pin it on you. That's the second
thing your secret pal has sent you, isn't
it?"

"Yep," said Robin. "And I still can't
guess who it is."

"Let's study the handwriting. That's

what detectives do." Jenny peered at the mailer. "It looks sort of shaky."

"Maybe an old person wrote it," said Robin. "My mom's secret pal was an old lady."

"Maybe," said Jenny. "Do you know any old ladies?"

Robin shook her head. "Just my grandma. I don't think *she'd* be my secret pal."

"Lunch!" called Mrs. Hill.

First they had English-muffin pizzas. Then came pear-half clowns. Each clown had raisin eyes, a cherry nose, and an apple-slice mouth. Its collar was cream cheese and its hat was a cookie.

"This is the best lunch I've ever had," said Jenny. "You're a terrific cook, Mrs. Hill."

She wasn't just being polite. Robin could tell. Then, as she finished her own clown, Robin had an idea.

"Everything seems to be wearing a

hat today," she said. "The donkey, the clowns—even you, Jenny, when you came over. Why don't we make hats for the Gumbo bears? We could use a paper plate for Big Gumbo and a margarine tub for Middle Gumbo—"

"And a Styrofoam cup for Little Gumbo," finished Jenny.

"You could decorate them too," said Mrs. Hill. "I have a whole bag of scraps."

"Great!" Jenny jumped up. "I'll go home and get the bears."

"I'll come with you," said Robin. "You can use my umbrella and I'll use Mom's. That way we can keep all the Gumbos dry."

A few minutes later they trudged up the O'Rourkes' back steps.

I've never been inside Jenny's flat before, thought Robin.

She waited in the kitchen while Jenny got the Gumbos. Other people's homes smell different from your own, she told herself. I don't like the smell here. It's sour.

"Need any help, Jenny?" she called.

"Shhh!" Jenny poked her head around the door. "My mom's resting. I'll be right there."

"Okay," whispered Robin. Why is she resting in the middle of the day? she wondered. Is she sick or something?

Come to think of it, she hardly ever saw Jenny's mother. Sometimes she came out on the porch to call Jenny. But that was all. Jenny's dad was *never* around.

I haven't said one word to Jenny's parents, thought Robin. They haven't said one word to me. Jenny never asks me over here to play either. That's sort of weird.

Later, she sat staring at a piece of yellow ribbon. It would look great on Little Gumbo's Styrofoam cup.

"What do you think?" Jenny held up Middle Gumbo's margarine tub. "Should

I paste on pink flowers or green feathers?"

Robin looked at the bear. Then she looked at Jenny. Her hair was a mess. She had a blob of paste on her nose. But her eyes were shining.

All at once Robin felt a soft, warm feeling deep inside. So what if her house smells bad and her parents act weird? she thought. Jenny's my *friend.*

"Both," she said. "And the yellow ribbon too."

E I G H T
The Green Ooblie

It rained for a whole week. Then at last the sun came out.

Just in time too, thought Robin. Today's the day Mom is taking me out to lunch at a fancy restaurant.

She was sitting on her back porch. Beside her sat her box of paper dolls. But she didn't feel like playing with them. She felt in a silly mood.

"Hi!" called Jenny from her porch. "Whatcha doing?"

"Taking up space." Robin giggled. "That's what my dad says sometimes."

She giggled again. "Hey, Jenny, did you ever smell your knees? They smell like sunshine."

Jenny bent over and sniffed. "You're right," she said. "I wonder if they smell like snow in winter."

"I don't know," said Robin. "I've never smelled them in winter." She giggled once more.

"Time to get dressed for lunch, Miss Laughing Hyena," said her mother. "I mean a *dress* too. If you like, you may invite Jenny to go with us. *If* it's all right with her mother."

"Super!" yelled Robin. "My mom says to ask your mom if you can go with us to a fancy restaurant. You have to wear a dress, though."

"Just a minute." Jenny hurried inside. "My mom doesn't care," she reported. "I'll be over as soon as I change."

"Jenny's mom doesn't care," Robin told her mother.

"I see." For a moment Mrs. Hill's mouth looked tight.

My mom doesn't like Jenny's mom, thought Robin. She pulled her pink-and-white sundress over her head. She probably thinks Jenny's mom *should* care more about her. I guess she's right. At least Jenny has *us.*

On the way to the restaurant, they left Danny at the baby-sitter's house.

"Poor old Curly," said Jenny. "No fancy restaurants for him."

"He doesn't care," said Robin. "He just wants his peanut butter and his Boop."

"Boop!" laughed Jenny. "That is the *craziest* name for a blanket."

"Did you ever notice how other words sound funny too?" Robin felt her silly mood coming back. "Especially if you say them over and over again? Like 'sleep.' I'll bet you can't say 'sleep' ten times without giggling."

Jenny couldn't.

"I've made reservations for a garden table," said Mrs. Hill at the restaurant. "Now, *please* try to act like civilized human beings."

They did pretty well too, thought Robin. At least until after their chicken-salad sandwiches. Then, out of nowhere, came the funniest, silliest, *dumbest* thought she had ever had.

She leaned over to Jenny. "A green ooblie is watching you," she whispered.

"What?" said Jenny.

"A green ooblie is watching you!" Robin exploded into giggles.

"A green ooo—" Jenny started giggling too.

"I don't believe this," said Mrs. Hill. "A green what?"

"Oo-oo-*ooblie!*" gasped Robin. "Oh, I can't stand it. I'm *dying!*"

Jenny sat up very straight. "I am not going to think about a green ooblie," she said. "I am not—ooo!"

51

She was off.

"I give up," said Mrs. Hill. "If you can't beat 'em, join 'em. Did you girls know that it is impossible to kiss your own elbow?"

"It is?" Robin tried. "Hey, it *is*!"

"But not for a gr-gr-green ooblie," said Jenny.

"Oh, no!" groaned Robin. "Here we go again."

It was the wildest lunch she'd ever had.

That evening she went grocery shopping with her parents and Danny. They were loading bags into the trunk when Robin stooped down.

"Look at this," she said. She held up a pink plastic heart charm. "How about that? I never found anything good before."

When she got home, she put the charm on a piece of yarn. Then she went out on the porch.

Maybe Jenny's out too, she thought. I can send my charm over in the basket to show her.

She peered across in the twilight. There sat Jenny. She was hugging one of the Gumbos.

She sure loves those bears, thought

Robin. Hey! I know what I'll do with the heart.

"Jenny!" she called. "Send Middle Gumbo over for a minute. I've got a surprise for you."

"Well—uh—okay," said Jenny.

Why does she sound so strange? thought Robin. The Gumbos have ridden back and forth lots of times.

She took Middle Gumbo out of the basket. She tied the heart charm around its neck. It made a perfect locket.

Then Robin noticed something. One side of Middle Gumbo's head was very wet.

But it's not raining, she thought. How—?

All at once Robin understood. Jenny had been hugging Middle Gumbo close to her face. And she'd been crying.

N I N E

Jenny's News

"Are—are you okay, Jenny?" asked Robin.

"Yeah, I'm okay." Jenny tried to laugh. "Any green ooblies over there?"

"Not right now." Robin put Middle Gumbo in the basket and pulled at the rope. "But here comes your surprise."

"Hey, terrific!" said Jenny. "The locket will match the flowers on her hat."

"That's what I thought," said Robin. "Well, good night, Jenny. See you tomorrow?"

"See you tomorrow."

Robin took a long time getting ready

for bed. She couldn't stop thinking about Jenny. At last her mother came into her room. She sat down on the edge of Robin's bed.

"What's the matter, honey?" she asked. "You don't look very happy."

"It's Jenny, Mom. She's been crying and I don't know why. I thought we had *fun* today."

"I see." Mrs. Hill sighed. "Well, Robin, I think Jenny did have fun today. In fact, I know she did. But I think she has some pretty big problems at home too."

"You mean her parents?" asked Robin. "They're kind of strange. At least her mom is. I've never met her dad."

"They're unhappy people, Robin. Their bedroom window is right across from ours, you know. Your father and I hear them arguing almost every night. I'm sure Jenny hears them too."

Robin nodded. "She does. Sometimes she can't sleep because of the fights. But what can I *do*, Mom? I want to help her."

"You can be her friend, honey." She patted Robin's hand. "You can listen to her and care about her. That's the best thing anybody can do."

"I think I'll say a prayer for her too," said Robin. "Dear God, please take care of my friend Jenny. Stop her parents from messing up her life. Amen."

Mrs. Hill stood up. "I love you, Robin," she said. "Good night."

"Thanks, Mom. Good night."

The next day Robin sent Jenny a picture she'd drawn of a green ooblie. But the picture just stayed in the basket. Jenny didn't even come out on the porch.

"Mom, have you seen Jenny this morning?" asked Robin.

"No, I haven't seen her," said Mrs. Hill. "Maybe she's busy."

"Maybe." Robin went into her room. She saw the card with flowers on her bul-

letin board. I wonder if I should be Jenny's secret pal, she thought. Would that cheer her up?

No, she decided. She'd guess right away I was doing it. Besides, we already send each other stuff all the time. I guess Mom is right. All I can do is be her friend. But that sure isn't easy when she isn't even around.

At last, right after lunch, she saw the basket on her side. In it was a note.

Meet me at the fence at three.
VERY important!

Jenny

Robin thought three o'clock would never come. She cleaned her room. She brushed Pottsy. She played with Danny. At ten to three she went downstairs. Maybe Jenny would be early too.

But she wasn't. When she did come, she was walking very slowly. In one hand she held Little Gumbo.

"I've got news, Robin," she said. "My folks are getting a divorce. We're leaving."

T E N

Three Wet Gumbos

"Leaving?" Robin felt as if she couldn't breathe. "You *can't* be."

"But we are." Jenny was almost whispering. "I was pretty sure last night. That's why I was crying. Then, today—" She stopped and looked around. "Isn't there someplace we can go, Robin? Someplace no one will see us?"

Robin thought. "There's the space between the garages. But we'll have to sit on the ground."

"That's okay." Jenny hurried into Robin's yard. "Come on."

60

They went between the garages and sat down in the dirt.

"Now *tell* me," said Robin. "Maybe you didn't really understand what your parents said."

"I understood, all right." Jenny took a deep breath. "They had the worst fight they've ever had. My dad said all my mom does is drink. My mom said it was his fault because he has a girlfriend. Then they started screaming all these horrible words."

"Wow!" said Robin. "It sounds like a TV program. Are you *sure* they decided to get a divorce?"

Jenny nodded hard. "Yep. My dad wants to marry this other girl. And my mom wants to go to Texas. N-neither one of them wants me."

Her eyes filled with tears. Robin didn't even stop to think. She just reached over and hugged her.

"Well, phooey on them, then!" she said. *"I* want you. Maybe we can get my parents to adopt you."

Jenny shook her head. "Aw, Robin, *that's* the kind of thing that only happens on TV." She glanced up toward her flat. "Right now my parents are up there trying to figure out what to do with me. Do—do you think it's my fault?"

"What?" asked Robin. "The *divorce*?"

"Yes." Jenny began to cry. "Maybe if I had been a better kid, it wouldn't have happened. I could have—"

All at once, Robin was furious.

"Jenny O'Rourke, don't you *dare* say that!" she yelled. "You're a *great* kid. Besides, kids don't make divorces happen. Grown-ups do. It's *their* dumb, stupid fault, not yours!"

She was crying too now. For a long time she and Jenny just sat there, hugging and crying. It seemed to be all they could do.

At last they heard someone calling.

"That's my mom," said Jenny. "I'd better go." She stood up.

"Can you come back later?" asked Robin.

"I don't know." Jenny smiled a sad little smile. "Look at Little Gumbo. He's all wet."

Robin tried to smile too. "Yesterday it was Middle Gumbo. Big Gumbo is the only dry bear you've got left."

"No, he isn't." Jenny giggled and sniffled at the same time. "I cried all over *him* last night. Poor Gumbos!"

Robin hugged her again. "I love you, Jenny," she said.

"I love you too, Robin." Jenny hugged her back. Then she turned and ran.

Slowly Robin went upstairs. She cried when she told her mother what had happened. Later, she cried when she told her father. But when she got into bed, she couldn't cry anymore.

"I'm going to say a different kind of prayer tonight," she said to her mother. "Dear God, I am really mad at You. I *asked* You to help Jenny. But You didn't do it. Now You'd just better work a miracle. Amen. Do you think that will make God mad at *me*, Mom?

"No, honey," said her mother. "I think God wants to know what you're feeling."

"Well, I'm feeling mad," said Robin. "And hurt." She began to cry again. "Oh, Mom, I never knew that being a friend could hurt so much!"

E L E V E N

The Message

The next morning Robin woke up late.
All that crying must have worn me out,
she thought. But for a moment she
couldn't remember why she had been
crying.

Then it all came back. Jenny! Jenny
was *leaving*!

"Mom! *Mom!*" she yelled. She jumped
out of bed and ran to the kitchen. "Mom,
has Jenny been looking for me?"

Her mother was sitting at the kitchen
table.

"No, Robin," she said. "Sit down a minute. I have something to tell you."

Robin sat down. Whatever her mother had to say wouldn't be good. Not when she used that voice. Robin held her breath.

"I'm sorry, honey," said her mother. "But Jenny is gone. They all left very early this morning."

"Oh, no, Mom," whispered Robin. "You must be wrong. Maybe they just went to the store. Maybe they'll come back in a little while."

"No." Mrs. Hill put her arm around Robin. "They had their suitcases with them."

"But Jenny wouldn't *do* that!" cried Robin. Surely her mother must understand. "She'd never leave without saying good-bye to me. She *wouldn't!*"

"Oh, Robin, I wish there were something I could say. I just don't—"

But Robin wasn't listening. "The basket!" she yelled. "I'll bet there's a message in the basket."

She ran out onto the porch. Sure

enough, the basket was on her side. Robin looked into it and gasped.

There lay Middle Gumbo, hat, locket, and all. A note was taped to her paw.

Dear Robin,

Guess what? I am going to live with my grandparents in Chicago! Isn't that terrific? I'm sorry that I couldn't see you. But I will write you a letter. Take good care of M.G. And thanks for being my friend.

Love,

Jenny

Robin went back inside. She showed the note to her mother.

"I guess that's the miracle," she said. "Jenny really loves her grandparents. And they love her too. I guess God knew that."

"I guess He did," said her mother.

"But, Mom, I'm going to miss her so *much*." Robin felt tears trickle down her face.

"I know, honey." Her mother handed her a tissue. "But you can write letters the way Gwen and I do. And it looks as if you have a very special bear to remember Jenny by."

"A Gumbo bear," said Robin. "She actually gave me one of her *Gumbo* bears. That's sort of like a miracle too." She sighed. "Well, I guess it will feel right at home here."

"What do you mean?" asked her mother.

Robin sighed again. "I cried all over it," she said. "Just like Jenny."

T W E L V E

Friends

For a few days Robin moped around the house. Then her parents sent her to visit Grandma Bennett again. By the time she came home, she felt better. But she still hadn't gotten a letter from Jenny.

"I can't write her first," she told her mother one morning. "I don't know her address."

"Just be patient, Robin," said Mrs. Hill. "I'm sure she'll write."

Maybe the mailman got here early today, thought Robin. I'll go check.

She clattered down the front steps and opened the door.

"*Achoo!*"

"Melissa!" said Robin. "What are *you* doing on our front porch?"

"This dumb allergy!" said Melissa. "I could have gotten away if I hadn't started sneezing. I forgot my pill again this morning."

"But what were you doing here in the first place?" asked Robin. "And what's that?"

She pointed to a big flat parcel on the floor.

"That?" said Melissa. "I don't know. I've never seen it before in my life."

She is trying to act innocent, thought Robin. But she isn't doing a very good job.

All at once she had an idea. She picked up the parcel and tore it open. Inside was a cardboard poster of a puppy. On the back was written, "To Robin from your Secret Pal."

"*You*, Melissa Berger!" shouted Robin. "*You're* my secret pal, aren't you?"

"Secret pal?" asked Melissa in her innocent voice. Then she turned pink and giggled. "Well, I guess I am."

"I don't believe it!" said Robin.

"I—I felt so bad about reading your diary," explained Melissa. "I just did it to see if you liked me. I mean, you were so *polite* all the time, I couldn't tell how you really felt."

"I was trying to make *you* like *me*," said Robin.

"Oh. Well, anyway, I felt so bad. So I thought I'd try to do nice things for you. Mostly I used the mail." She pointed to the poster. "But this was too big. I brought it over on my bike. I—I guess I sort of hoped you'd catch me. Then maybe we could be friends again."

"I don't believe it," said Robin again. "I mean, sure, we can be friends. Come on upstairs. I can hardly wait to tell my mom it was you all along."

"That was a very sweet thing for you

to do, Melissa," said Mrs. Hill. "Why don't you ask your mother if you can stay for lunch? We'll celebrate the end of the secret."

Melissa stayed all afternoon. She and Robin played jacks, hopscotch, and Chinese checkers.

"My mom is taking me to buy school stuff tomorrow," said Melissa. "Pencils and things. Want to come along?"

"Sure," said Robin. "Is it really almost time for school?"

"It really is," said Melissa.

"I don't believe it," said Robin.

The next morning she got a letter from Jenny. It was on bright-yellow paper.

Dear Robin,

Well, here I am in Chicago. My grandparents are being wonderful. They got me a calico kitten. Her name is Sara Marlena. They take me places too. Yesterday we went to a fancy restaurant. But there were no green ooblies.

I miss you a lot, Robin. My grandma says you should come visit me sometime. Would you? Please write me a letter.

Your friend forever,
Jenny

Robin read the letter four times. Her heart felt very full. So she got out her diary. She set Middle Gumbo on her desk in front of her. Then she wrote:

Dear Diary,

Summer is almost over. I have been busy. That is why I have not written much. It has been a happy and a sad summer. I made the best friend ever. Then she had to leave. Now Melissa Berger and I are friends again. But Jenny will be my best friend forever. And I will never forget my Jenny summer.